The Elephant
and the Bad Baby

Story by Elfrida Vipont

Illustrations by Raymond Briggs

Coward-McCann, Inc. / New York

Copyright © 1969 by Elfrida Vipont
Copyright © 1969 by Raymond Briggs
All rights reserved.
First published in Great Britain 1969 by
Hamish Hamilton Children's Books.
First American edition 1969.
Reissued 1986.
First paperback edition 1986.
Printed in Hong Kong by South China Printing Co.
Library of Congress Cataloging-in-Publication Data
Vipont, Elfrida, 1902-
The elephant and the bad baby.
Summary: Whenever the bad baby wants
something the big elephant gets it for him.
[1. Behavior—Fiction]   I. Briggs, Raymond, ill.
II. Title.
PZ7.V817E   1986   [E]   85-15004
ISBN 0-698-20039-X
ISBN 0-698-20625-8 (pbk.)

Once upon a time there was an Elephant.

One day the Elephant went for a walk and met a Bad Baby.
And the Elephant said to the Bad Baby, "Would you like a ride?"
And the Bad Baby said yes.

So the Elephant stretched out his trunk,
picked up the Bad Baby, and put him on his back.
And they went rumpeta, rumpeta, rumpeta, all down the road.

Soon they met an ice cream man.
And the Elephant said to the Bad Baby, "Would you like an ice cream?"
And the Bad Baby said yes.

So the Elephant stretched out his trunk and took an ice cream for himself and an ice cream for the Bad Baby.

And they went rumpeta, rumpeta, rumpeta, all down the road, with the ice cream man running after.

Next, they came to a butcher's shop.
And the Elephant said to the Bad Baby, "Would you like a meat pie?"
And the Bad Baby said yes.

So the Elephant stretched out his trunk and took a pie for himself
and a pie for the Bad Baby.

And they went rumpeta, rumpeta, rumpeta, all down the road,
with the ice cream man and the butcher both running after.

Next, they came to a baker's shop.
And the Elephant said to the Bad Baby, "Would you like a bun?"
And the Bad Baby said yes.

So the Elephant stretched out his trunk and took a bun for himself and a bun for the Bad Baby.

And they went rumpeta, rumpeta, rumpeta, all down the road, with the ice cream man, and the butcher, and the baker all running after.

Next, they came to a snackshop.
And the Elephant said to the Bad Baby, "Would you like some gingersnaps?"
And the Bad Baby said yes.

So the Elephant stretched out his trunk and took some gingersnaps for
himself and some gingersnaps for the Bad Baby.

And they went rumpeta, rumpeta, rumpeta, all down the road, with the
ice cream man, and the butcher, and the baker, and the snackshop man
all running after.

Next, they came to a grocery store.
And the Elephant said to the Bad Baby, "Would you like a chocolate cookie?"
And the Bad Baby said yes.

So the Elephant stretched out his trunk and took a chocolate cookie
for himself and a chocolate cookie for the Bad Baby.

And they went rumpeta, rumpeta, rumpeta, all down the road,
with the ice cream man, and the butcher, and the baker,
and the snackshop man, and the grocer all running after.

Next, they came to a candy store.
And the Elephant said to the Bad Baby, "Would you like a lollipop?"
And the Bad Baby said yes.

So the Elephant stretched out his trunk and took a lollipop
for himself and a lollipop for the Bad Baby.

And they went rumpeta, rumpeta, rumpeta, all down the road,
with the ice cream man, and the butcher, and the baker,
and the snackshop man, and the grocer, and the lady
from the candy store all running after.

Next, they came to a fruit and vegetable stand.
And the Elephant said to the Bad Baby, "Would you like an apple?"
And the Bad Baby said yes.
   So the Elephant stretched out his trunk and took an apple for himself
and an apple for the Bad Baby.
   And they went rumpeta, rumpeta, rumpeta, all down the road,
with the ice cream man, and the butcher, and the baker,
and the snackshop man, and the grocer, and the lady from the candy store,
and the fruit and vegetable man all running after.

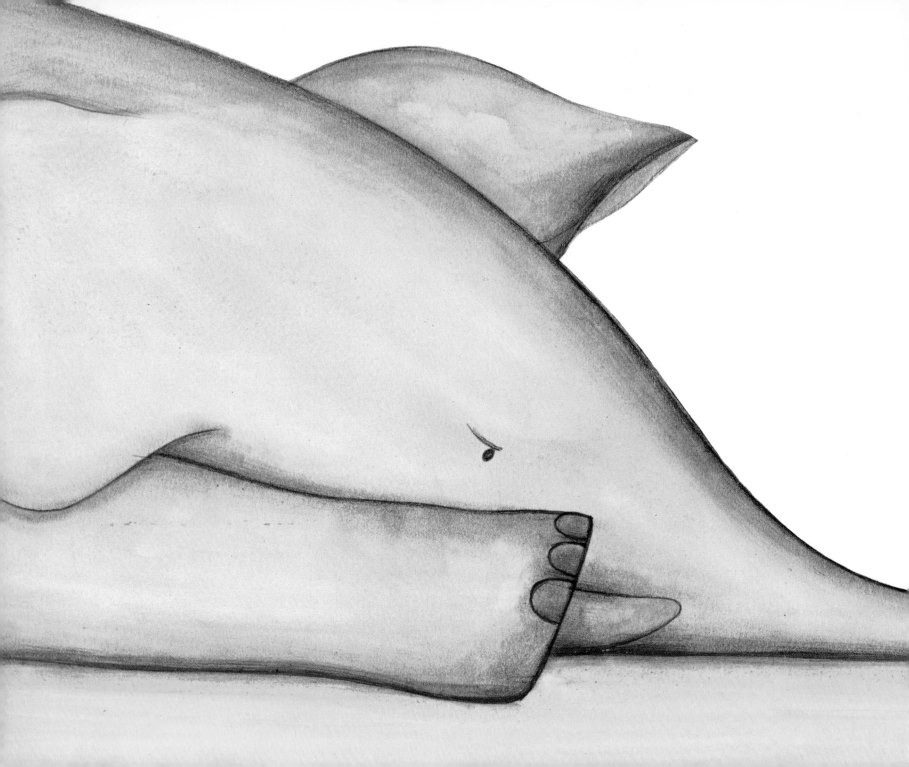

Then the Elephant said to the Bad Baby,
"But you haven't once said please!"
And then he said, "You haven't ONCE said please!"
    Then the Elephant sat down suddenly in the middle
of the road, and the Bad Baby fell off.

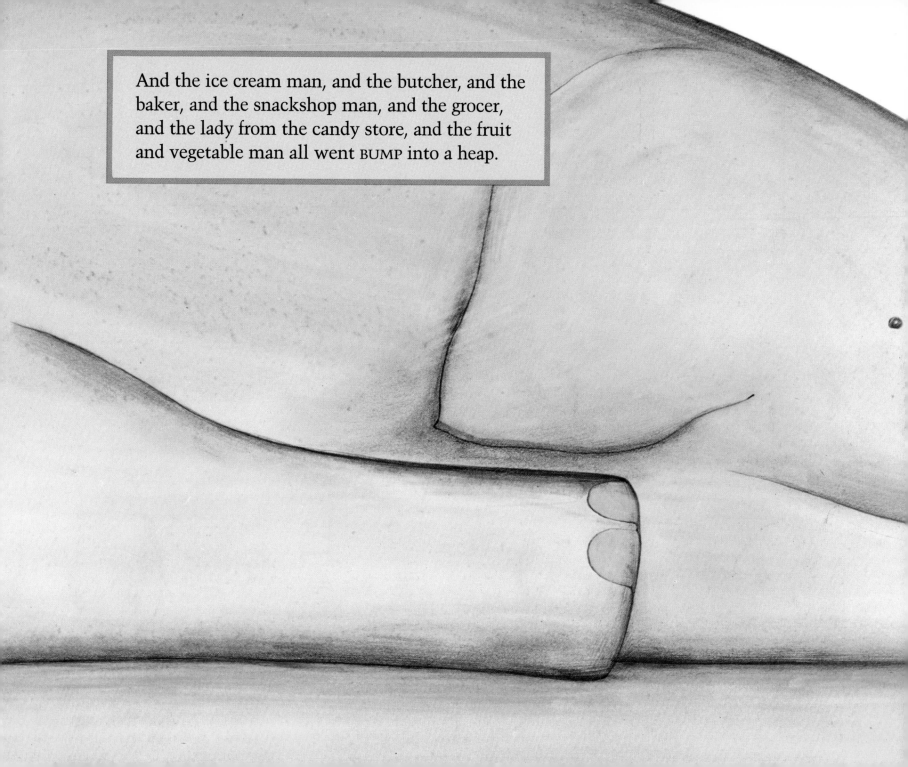

And the ice cream man, and the butcher, and the baker, and the snackshop man, and the grocer, and the lady from the candy store, and the fruit and vegetable man all went BUMP into a heap.

And the Elephant said, "He never once said please!"

  And the ice cream man, and the butcher, and the baker, and the snackshop man, and the grocer, and the lady from the candy store, and the fruit and vegetable man all picked themselves up and said, "Just imagine that! He never once said please!"

And the Bad Baby said, "PLEASE! I want to go home to my mother."

So the Elephant stretched out his trunk, picked up the Bad Baby, and put him on his back.

And they went rumpeta, rumpeta, rumpeta, all down the road, with the ice cream man, and the butcher, and the baker, and the snackshop man, and the grocer, and the lady from the candy store, and the fruit and vegetable man all running after.

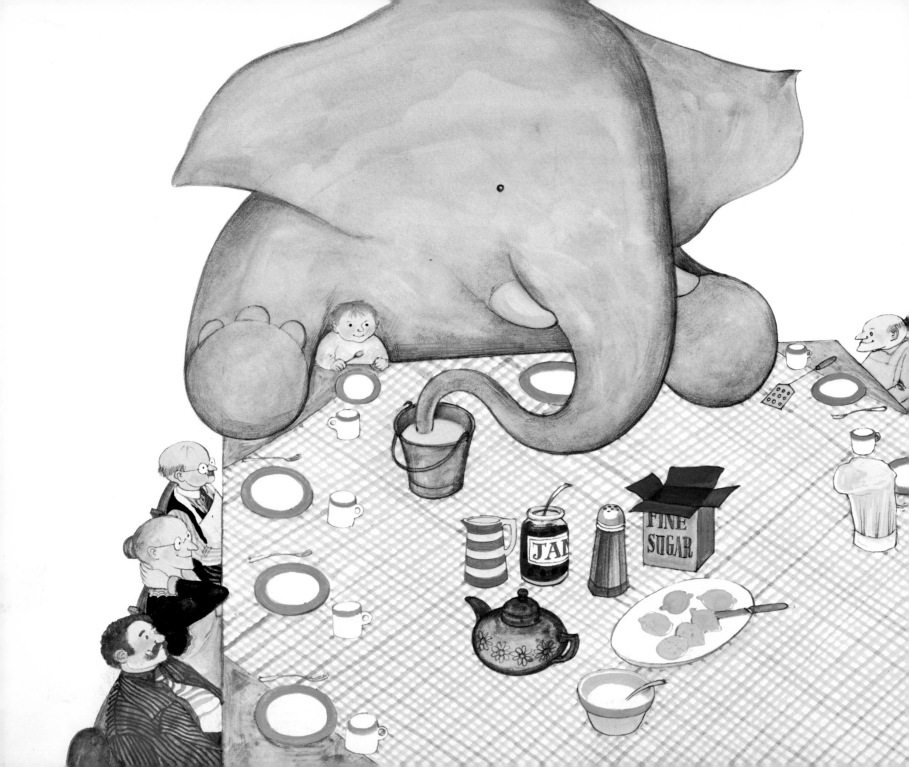

When the Bad Baby's mother saw them, she said, "Have you all come for supper?"

And the Bad Baby said, "Yes, PLEASE!"

So they all went in and had supper, and the Bad Baby's mother made pancakes for everybody.

Then the Elephant went rumpeta, rumpeta, rumpeta, all down the road, with the ice cream man, and the butcher, and the baker, and the snackshop man, and the grocer, and the lady from the candy store, and the fruit and vegetable man all running after.

But the Bad Baby went to bed.